926 YEARS

926 Years

KYLE COMA-THOMPSON

TRISTAN FOSTER

A SUBLUNARY OBJECT

ISBN 978-0-578-57035-8
Library of Congress Control Number: 2019951124

Manufactured in the United States of America
Printed on acid-free paper
First published by Sublunary Editions in 2019
Design and typesetting by Joshua Rothes

Sublunary Editions
2400 NW 80th Street #206
Seattle, WA 98117
sublunaryeditions.com

CONTENTS

926 YEARS

It is said children still have a sense of wonder, later one becomes blunted. —Nonsense. A child takes things for granted, and most people get no further; only an old person, who thinks, is aware of the wondrous.

Victor Klemperer
January 1, Thursday (1942)

The child is dying. The daughter, eight years old. He's worked for the Center twenty years and has made this very drive to Amish country at least once a season. This family, though. One of the hardest. The father a carpenter. His youngest born with Tay-Sachs. Paralysis, seizures. The gene pool so narrow in these kinds of communities, he would never say it, higher rate of birth defects. Easier to talk sociology than stand and hold the hand of a pale girl in her jammies, dying because God must want her to. The room's fresh and bright, two big windows. Outside it's July and the girl will never walk again. He says his prayers. He steps out into the hallway. No one in the common room. Looks around. A work bench in the adjoining room. Surprised: power tools laying around here and there, extension cords of every color. When the father comes around, Chaplain Blake asks: how do you run these, if you don't use electricity out here? The father takes him around back and there he sees something so unlikely it could very well be a lie, now, as he remembers it. Two horses trotting on handmade treadmills. Here he's trained them to walk through the day and churn the gears and charge a generator, which in turn brings the blessing of 100% organic electricity to his drill and saw. That way, he explains, he is able to make more better and faster, so

1

he can sell them. All the better to afford the best care for Carollee. Later that summer, Chaplain B will have an intern riding along, for a return visit. "Your parents are your first gods," he tells the college kid. "And if they disappoint you…"

The body man watched the great man read a $5.99 Dalai Lama biography, its cover a photo of the subject smiling and in sunglasses, snow-capped Himalayas behind him. Finished the final pages as the plane came in to land. Touched down with a single hop before smoothing out and slowing to a driveway crawl. The great man closed the book, held it in his hands, as if in thanks, then tucked it into the pouch in front of him, where he would leave it. "Getting old," he said. "Next Dalai won't be found in China's territories. There may not even be another Lama. Smart boy. The last of his species. The last to be reincarnated, the magic trick dying with him." His body man asked: "According to him?" The great man grinned. "Well, he'd know," he said. "Smart boy." He brushed out his robe, picked some lint off the bright fabric, exhaled deeply. Better rested than usual after the long flight. Mood was up. Relieved the great man would be at his best this morning and, if he was lucky, the rest of the trip. Cabin manager approached, suit crisp and cologned, leaned in for privacy. "Sir, we've been told there is a large crowd waiting for you. There is even a crowd at the gate." Looked at the body man. "Is there anything we can do to assist?" The great man smiled. "Please inform them I am coming and that I am honored and excited to see them," he said. The two joked, each enjoying the other's attention. It never failed to impress the body man—the great man brought engagement and excitement like no one he'd ever met. When the cabin manager had left to give his message, the great man turned to look behind him, as if he'd be able to see through the curtain separating first class from the rest of the plane. "I hope Pierre is ready," he said. Before he stepped off the plane, Pierre would tidy up the great man for his acolytes while he stood there like a young prince. He would be made up, his bright teeth checked, his long nails cleaned, his silver-dyed hair combed and his beard brushed out. Probably brought another glass of champagne by a hostess, which he would take graciously though not drink. The great man loved every moment of it. "It's a beautiful, beautiful day," said the great man. "We must give thanks that we are alive to enjoy it."

The *teisho* will be recorded some twenty years earlier. The twenty years will pass, cause and effect will spin its ephemeral web, catching days and weeks and months like flies—flies of no certain spider. In a well-lit room Rosalice will sit cross-legged, both feet gone numb. Six other strangers doing their Buddha best, and Roshi Merete pressing play on her smartphone. Bluetooth to a portable speaker set among trinkets and incense on the altar. Everyone's gaze is focused roughly two inches from where their ankles cross, on the carpet. Tape hiss, hollow acoustics, a moth caught under a hi-ball glass, sounds just like that—patting frantically against the curves of a transparent interior. Another roshi, this one with an accent. Hard to place. German. No wait, Brazilian. Could be the confluence of several tongues into ambiguously destabilized English. There are sniffles, coughs, people in the background, twenty-year-old phantom people. The recorded roshi's voice is kind but firm, how you'd expect. And says this: Much as the geese and other such birds at the beginning of the winter months fly south towards more inviting climates, it's the nature of human beings to move in unconscious arrow formation as well. They take turns, leading the pack. The burden of cutting resistance through the air, something they share. Others fly, you see, in the wake; and that is why they form a V. The wake makes for easy flying, particularly at the furthest, outermost edges. The ones in the rear work less, conserve strength, eventually make their way towards the top of the V, tip of the arrow, then when it's time and the leader has tired, assume the vanguard position. It is written into them by instinct to share the effort, burrowing southwards through the sky; that neverending sky we all live below. Rosalice and six others, plus Roshi Merete. Twenty years now far behind them, this room lucid with seven o'clock summer sunlight. When it's time, another twenty will move out ahead of them, then another. Then they'll fall behind, and rest.

A flare of sansho pepper on the tongue tip. Catch the tree at the right time of year and the fruit bursts, raining peppercorns down. Maybe like the season when pistachios open, the night snapping like broken locust song. Used for seasoning eel. Sansho leaves for garnishing fish. Clap it between the hands for aroma, make a wish, the finishing touch to the perfect soup. In Korea, the unripe fruit was used for fishing. Poisonous to the smallest ones. That was cheating wasn't it? Or was pulling up a fish all that mattered? Xuthus swallowtail laid its perfect, caviar eggs on the leaves, the larvae hatching to eat up its edges and one day bursting into a second life among its branches. Used color vision for foraging. Population of the butterfly was kept stable by a genus of parasitic wasp. When the number of butterflies increased, the wasp multiplied to match. The life of the wasps were shorter than that of the butterflies, so their number rose until they achieved butterfly equilibrium then died back down in pointless and eternal harmony. The pepper one of six magical ingredients in Japanese gin. Could taste its spice in a sip. Especially on quiet nights. Like tonight. New bar, same lost, of course. Put away a few gin and tonics, taking shelter in the known. Pepper on the tongue and gin in the bloodstream so one thing led to another led to another. Caught the eyes of men as usual. Single drinkers, sitting around the bar, thirsty in more ways than one. Preferred to think about the tiny wasp, so small it could barely fit enough neurons in its body to operate. Or the butterfly—what a world—zebra-striped but blessed with color vision. Or the way that primates developed color vision to distinguish ripe food or predators or emotions in other angry or sad primates. Like thirsty men across the bar. One of them finished his drink and stood and approached her booth. Patterned shirt, tucked into trousers, spectacles and a dad haircut. Wedding band stashed away, probably. Dick basically useless. Said something to her which she either didn't understand or didn't listen to. The ancient Greeks called non-speakers of Greek βάρβαρος—the blah blahs. Became, in English, in time, *barbarian*. Waved away the blah blah. Finished the last drink and crunched on the ice and turned up the empty glass on the table. A sign to fight in some cultures, a sign to leave now. Walked the night. Walked and walked, shoes biting, stopping, finally, in the neon light of a deserted petrol station.

You can track his travel route by languages acquired. As he'll tell you, English was only the final destination. Before Phoenix, London; before London, Barcelona; before that, Genoa, Milan, a dribble of Italian addresses further, further south. From Cairo, a reach backwards across the north to Dakar, where his first two tongues were born—French and Wolof. This much he brought with him like luggage, eight ways of talking, to a city named after a bird that self-combusts for the sake of rebirth. And get this. The first job he lands there? Third shift janitor at Sky Harbor International. An airport. Who'd take to the sky from a place that leaps to flight from its own flames? Dax, his supervisor, assigns him Concourse B. Two other guys on shift. They talk shit through the night over walkie-talkies. They warned him and he thought, They joking. There's a spook who hides out in bathrooms. The Weeper, they call him. Babukar assumes they're just ribbing the newbie. But no—if only. Because isn't it true one night, way late, about four in the A.M., he parks his cleaning cart outside the bathroom between Gates 23 and 24, rolls in his mop and bucket, steps in and immediately hears moaning and sniffling. Someone in the bathroom. Scares him all the way back to French and Wolof. *Qui est là?* he asks. No answer. *Na nga def?* A long minute passes. The door to the furthest stall opens and a guy in a brown suit steps out, edges to the sink. Turns on both faucets, hot and cold, and instead of pumping soap in his hands, turns heel and walks towards him, towards him and past him, sink still running. The look on the face. Babukar'd find it hard to describe. That's him, the guys later tell him. Yep, there he blows. The resident spook. A man-sized ghost, they allege, or maybe just a sleepwalker. Always in the early morning, always sobbing, always in stalls furthest from the door. Next time I see him, B promises, I'll grab him, give him a shake. See what comes of him, if I wake him. No one agrees it's a good idea. Turns out, as he'll learn, that's the last thing he should do. Never wake a sleepwalker unless you know for sure he's a sleepwalker.

The endocrinologist could find nothing, the neurologist, the hematologist, the rheumatologist. They'd paid all this money, flown all this way, the Mayo Clinic, the past four months in a wheelchair, her husband pushing her around. Her husband driving her out to the river, to sit with her on a bench and watch the water and barges move along at an even pace, like years. Couldn't walk, couldn't lift her arms, no energy. Dr. Hess suggested they meet with Dr. Adebisi. "A psychologist?" her husband asked. Who needed a psychologist when they had a priest? But a visit to Dr. Adebisi would be covered in the costs, so they agreed. After asking her husband to wait outside, the kind man sat with her, asked questions and listened for half an hour, then after a pause of quiet consideration, said: *depression, PTSD*, words she never thought had much to do with her. He mentioned her husband and Vietnam. He mentioned fits of anger, her mother, childhood, poverty. And as an illustration of the point described to her a study done years ago. Mice were placed in cages. An aroma of cherry blossoms was pumped into the air and each time there were cherry blossoms, electric currents coursed through the metal floor of the cages. These mice had children. Those children had children. Three, four, five generations. As far as seven generations. They'd go about their day in their cages until the scent of cherry blossoms began wafting in. Though these mice had never been shocked, had never suffered themselves, they tensed and scrambled at the first hint of cherry. Fear, pain, it was born with them, they bore it without knowing, and this, Dr. Adebisi said to Mrs. Anderson, is perhaps why you are here today, in this wheelchair. Who else could I have been, she wondered, still feeling weak but also a bit sheepish, hours later, on the plane. Looking out her little window over the last tinseling leftovers of Minneapolis. Tiny lights, traffic coursing down an interstate. Some trace of an answer, the stronger part of her down in her weaker parts said. What's that? Not cherry blossoms, no. The tang of sweat on her husband's forearm.

Lie face down on the floor. High-gloss parquet in herringbone. Middle of the room. Others had had similar ideas. Put your head against the wall and think of a certain subject. Or lie down and look up, to think or to play with your smartphone, spend as long as you like—there were a lot of those. It was playful, a necessary break from the stuffiness and seriousness beyond the gallery doors. She spoke to her tour groups with enthusiasm and watched for reactions—she was a reaction person. The reactions of others were more valuable to her than her own. Liked going to the beach to see others laughing as cold waves engulfed them. Actually got a thrill when she told the group to lie down and there was resistance. She told them that was, in fact, the point. Press your face into the floor, into everything that the floor is. Consider, maybe, the materials used, where they came from, how they got here, the essence of the word *floor*, the fact gravity was keeping it pinned to the earth. If the world stopped spinning there was no reason everything should stay put. That tears don't run down cheeks in space. Spoke slowly, used her school teacher tone. Think of the trail of others who had come before you. The paths they had walked before they passed through here and where they went when they left. Not an easy thing. It was an exercise, really, in empathy. Liked seeing eyes widen when she told the resistant among them they had intuited the force of the work. Then there were those that refused to participate altogether. Would not get on the floor, crying discomfort, even disgust. She tucked her folio under her arm and smiled at them. What was their own hygiene like? Was their home spotless? Smelling of disinfectant? Or were they posturing? She didn't tell them cleaners came in every few hours and nobody had said this to her but she thought of their cleaning as part of the artwork. A critical part; maybe—and not that she yet understood why entirely—its secret, obverse side. The last group of the morning, before the doors were locked and the cleaners came through. Everybody had risen from the floor, amusement having faded, except for one man. Turned onto his back but stayed where he was while the others gravitated towards the next room. "Can I help you up, sir?" She hurried over. "Are you OK?" He didn't look like he was from here, bearded, wearing a cap with flaps, a tourist who had come on a cruise liner, she thought. He took a deep breath. The others on the tour began to gather around. He told them this reminded him of something and it had knocked the air out of him. Inhaled again. It had reminded him of a moment in a childhood that wasn't his.

Sick, to think people locked themselves in the dark, to get divine. Those medieval churches. Any light that reached them had to pass through rose windows. Take those churches by the spires, lift them up, let the people breathe. Full sky, atmosphere running wild. There's that song, "Are You Ready for the Country?" Country music, down near the roots, the pain of it speaks clarity, primitive knowledge. Class division runs like the sharpest knife, cuts the gristle off hardship. He always hated that he belonged to it. The sappy backwardness of it. The obsolete concerns that killed its many singers and shored their remains up on the radio as so many boring guitars. But he's country, there's no arguing. He's sitting in the backyard, isn't he? In a lawn chair? It's hours into the dark half of life and he's out there listening to the breeze play over the flush green leaves of the corn. It's about waist high. He can't see much of it. Just a lazy mass of stalks and leaves in Rorschach composure, right there before him. There's a bottle of *reposado* at the end of his reach, to his right. Bottle lifted from the grass to his lips, then set back, quite gently. The stars way high, like his forebears. Fireflies gaming about in the fields. In the far distance are the real beauties, three, no, five radio towers scattered about the horizon way out elsewhere in Pearl County.

People live out there. People no one will ever know about. In their trailers, in the teeth of circumstances no one begrudges them, that they're born with. They grow them like hands and feet. They reach out with them, touch each other with them. He's driven those roads way out there. Passed those stations. In the dark the towers show themselves by the pulsing of red lights that mark their heights. The lights there to signal: here be towers. So no low-flying plane might strike them. Why does it feel lonely, sitting and watching? Nature in its subtle power and monotony, pre-Internet to the core, unconscious of its enormity. No one. No one knows he's even here. The house at his back. Divorced. His ex elsewhere, how he loved her, hurt her, himself. Why's it beautiful, why's it comforting, that no one knows? The crickets bleeping in the grass around him, the corn growing before him. Far lights pulsing like heartbeats, waiting for lives and bodies to grow around. Loneliness, it's inarguable isn't it? Crowns a person like some kind of common wisdom. Then overthrows him.

Helpdesk on 11. Hell-pdesk was the old joke, hellllpdesk the new one. Sebastian wasted the morning, then the afternoon. Avoided calls, ignored chats, slow on the emails. Went to the park to breathe, reclining under a fig tree even if the day was wet. At drinks the night before, he had confessed to Anil, colleague but mainly friend, that he was having a hard time of it. Not feeling himself. Anil, tie loosened, regarded him sincerely and asked him what he meant. Considered admitting he was feeling what he could only describe as depressed, but Anil's response was enough to ease Sebastian's mind, at least a little, but enough, and he could drop it. The fig wasps worked despite the weather. Spied one and then saw all the others, telegraphing from tree to tree. To the next fig tree to the next. They drew invisible lines from each, searching the fruit like they were looking for a secret, until all the fig trees in the city were joined by their flights, mapped behind their fig wasp eyes. The tree creaked under its own weight. Swept the ground with its lowest hanging branches. Sebastian collected a few of the fruits, hands becoming sticky from sap, ants running up his wrists. Thumbing them in his pockets as he walked back to the office. Into the chattering and the keyboard clatter and neon lights. Crisped air and the distant scent of sugary energy drinks. Wall monitors with service scores flashing. Attracted a certain type and was conscious of this now. Didn't it. Came in one morning with this knowledge and couldn't shake it, that there was something about him that didn't fit, not anymore, and not just because his back was sometimes wet and his pockets bulging with inedible fruits. Felt young and stuck and old and free and was very possibly none of those things. Made him profoundly, deathly tired. Boss was in the islands with the family, sending photos from a yacht by group email like they were all friends. Got the Photoshop treatment. Surfing on a shark. At the base of a volcano. On the shoulder of Christ the Redeemer. By the Door to Hell in Turkmenistan. Worse from there, not safe for work.

This may sound like storytelling but it's the godless truth, Minda tells Devonte. He'd asked how work was going and though she was four months into motherhood, not just dog tired but mother-tired, she burst back into her old feral brightness. Well through her pregnancy and now beyond, she'd been working a case, defending a hospital whose name will, for purposes of this conversation, go unmentioned. Here's what happened. A hippie gets pregnant; she gets herself a doula; plans on a home birth. When her water breaks, they get her in a bathtub. No epidural, mind you. Straight natural pain for Hippie Momma. She and Doula get through thirty, thirty-six, forty hours of this and eventually the anguish breaks her. Doula drives her to the nearest E.R., they get her in and push her through labor. Mom gets released and goes home. In her care, per her request, she brings the afterbirth. Mom and Dad cook it up and eat it like veal. With a side of kale and sriracha. One week later they get a call from the hospital: "Mrs. So-And-So, we found it, the afterbirth, we have it here, clearly labeled, ready for you to pick up." Turns out, they mixed up afterbirths. Gave the Hippies the wrong slime! Some other poor baby's afterbirth. The shock, it's horrible. They're cannibals, right? Cannibals once-removed, at least. So what can they do? They sue the hospital. Here I come in, and oh god, the irony! Here I am preggers through all of this. Defending the hospital. Not much to be done. The Hippies win. And here's what's awesome. They get their money, sure. But what else is stipulated in the decision? Along with the payout, they get rights to the afterbirth, which, by this time, mind you, is A YEAR OLD. Right now, that's just where I came from, like, toDAY. The final meet-up. We had them sign an agreement. Stating: should they eat the afterbirth, and should they get ill, the hospital is no way culpable. That, my friend, is pure metaphor. The bared teeth of pure horrorhood and hilarity, Life. That's mine, right there. Yours?

Sushi chef from Korea. Enthusiastic *irasshaimase* despite that when the bell behind the door tinkled. Didn't even look up to see if the customer was coming or going. Yujun was best in the restaurant with a blowtorch. Blowtorched everything. Return customers demanded him, and something scorched. Thought for a time of being the best sushi maker on the globe. These are the things that come to us in quiet moments. Till we dismiss them for laziness, distracted by more trivial things. Anyway, no one who matters cares about the blowtorch. Mastered the wrong tool. Read manga and smoked cigarettes in bed as the morning sun cut in. Put his uniform on and tied his checkerboard bandana around his forehead, above his glasses. Got in early for prep. Sharpened knives, boiled rice, cleaned to a two-year-old *K-pop Hits* playlist. Joked with Hinata, the only Japanese waitress who worked at the restaurant, without quite flirting. Closed sign flipped to Open at 11. Yujun took his place at his station and started on some eel nigiri for the showcase. The door opened and the bell tinkled. Irasshaimase, they all said. A woman, older, entered and sat at the bar, directly in front of Yujun. Eyes met, then he continued making nigiri. He had seen her before, not the kind of person that typically wanted sushi as early as this, if at all, but this was that kind of neighborhood. She was older, at the tail end of middle age, deep wrinkles from too much sun in youth, little eyes. Wore a striped shirt and shorts like a teenage boy. Squinted at the menu, as if it wasn't in her language, when she ordered from Hinata. Thanked her kindly, touching her on the arm, motherly, then watched Yujun while she waited. She smiled at him when he looked up. Asked if he was in love, because he worked like he was. Said she didn't see love much anymore. "Love that was true. Back when, you heard about a crime of passion every other day. Every other week is maybe more accurate. We'd be at a funeral or trial for someone related to Dougie and those boys. Dougie out the front of the courthouse or the crematorium if it was bad with the dogs standing watch because he wasn't allowed in. Three Dobermann Pinschers that walked slow and awkward like giraffes. Fearsome because of their size but harmless. Some bloke had bashed his missus because he came home early and, well, you know. The age old story. Or he'd had a skin-full and went home and one thing led to another. Wrong-headed, of course, crazy, but it was love."

In bed, hot, so she kicks the covers off her legs. Next to Anika, god, her metabolism, it's fucking nuclear! Winter nights she heats the whole room... but summer? Walks into the house and everything's short of catching fire! Before she conked out, Anika told her about this thing she'd been obsessed about when she was a kid. Back when Russia was a big deal, they had this research station way down in Antarctica. There was this huge lake locked a couple of miles under the ice. The Russians had started drilling down towards it decades ago and no one knew what would come of it; people said the water down there hadn't been exposed to air for millions of years. What kind of bacteria was swimming around below the ice, itching to get out? The drill struck wet; pressure sucked ancient water a mile or so up the hole, where it froze again. Gave her a weird feeling, thinking about that lake. There were people like that, I mean, *she* was like that. Laying in the dark waiting for The Merciful Hormone to secrete from the more primitive parts of her brain... then the involuntary collages, dream to nightmare to dream. Mr. Brownstone, their kitty, they'd had to declaw him. Kept pouncing on Anika's eyes as she slept. The eyes flitting and rolling around, R.E.M. and such. Mr. Brownstone mistook it for a game. Anika with scratches on her cheeks in the morning. The whole bit about nine lives. Funny. Presupposes resurrection. The conviction she'll wake with, where's it come from? Clinging to the twist of sheets like it was some chunk of bean stalk she'd chopped down, in the middle of climbing it. That she's carrying within her countless lives, each waiting to break free of her. Twenty, thirty, a thousand, a hundred thousand different people just itching to continue the rest of what she'll never finish. Death as travel. Ontological adventure. Death as spy-work across time. The scratches on Anika's cheeks, faintly still there. When she squints, they don't fade out. No, they get clearer, darker. Show more. Tally marks. Lives taken? Given.

There was a cow on the road. Standing in the middle, as if it had been crossing and, by some divine force, stopped, legs frozen, unable to take another step. Black or dark brown, it watched him, watched his idling car, then turned away. He leaned on the horn again. The cow didn't look this time. He revved the engine, flashed his lights, edged closer, but it ignored him—this is where it would stay until the end of time. He reversed, giving himself space, then manoeuvred around the cow's rear. Finally clear, he hit the accelerator and continued on his way, the cow shrinking in the rearview. The cabin was old and stuffy, small, a double bed in the middle of the room. Black and white photos of nothing in particular on the walls, tiny kitchen with a buzzing bar fridge, sink and two-burner stove top. A television with a tower of VCRs next to it, the covers scratched, corners white from being moved or handled. Bathroom to the side. He pulled the curtains open and let the light in—at least it had a view: wide, sparkling river. He had the idea that there was an outdoor jacuzzi and a canoe in case he wanted to go for a paddle. But now that he saw the river, twinkling like a newborn universe, he imagined skipping everything and staring at this and this alone for the next few days. Felt, then, justified in his decision to come here. Isolate himself.

He was about to turn away when he noticed: a fire burned across the river. Thick smoke rising out of the greenery and pluming into the sky. For a moment his brain refused to register it. Then fear came. Then he felt at ease: he needed this. Watched the smoke gather and rise. Watched for long enough to feel like he had done it, or that it was part of the landscape. Six days before he'd received a text that read *I didn't make it* and he still hadn't recovered. Couldn't eat, couldn't sleep. Barely held it together in conversations, found himself a couple of times in a toilet cubicle sobbing into his hands, and soon knew he had to leave. To take a break to understand it. Why did he feel changed? *I didn't make it*. He didn't respond. There was no response, it just was. He carried it now, dazed and off balance, a misstep away from a vertiginous tumble.

Lew Wade Wiley •·····························• age 55

Something read, creepy, ever heard of the man? Wrote the longest diary known to history. Spoiled heir of the Prudentia fortune. The kind of perversity that could only occur in Boston. Rented out the top two floors of the most storied hotel in the city, curtains drawn through the day, opened only in the evening. The walls padded to muffle noise rising like steam from the streets below. Had so little to do with his time, he'd put ads in the papers asking for people to sit and talk with him. Would pay for their visit. Yes, this on the tail of the big craze for psychoanalysis. And there he'd sit with pen and paper, ask them about their lives, their worst fears, desires, the messy embarrassments of their commonalities, write it down, have the house person downstairs pay them with an envelope, and inside the envelope, past heads of state reincarnated as grubby slips of paper. Never give them new bills, he instructed, only old ones. Once they told him their lives, rights were signed over. An actual written contract. So the door closed behind them in a hungry way, their pasts sold. These he worked into undead monotone prose, the diary of Lew Wade Wiley, and so lived fuller than anyone who'd opened a newspaper to read those advertisements, wrote to that listed address, knocked at his penthouse door. In classic fashion, some were paid extra, to fuck him. Laid down with a bony hypochondriac diary, nothing else. In the end, when he fit the pistol in his mouth, popped his head like a firecracker, off the seeds went, spiraling. Flicks of lives spoken, then stolen into a turgidness unending. Fluttered down from on high over Harvard Square and elsewhere, money they'd used to buy food, pay rent, get sex, suck bottle, invest. In what—stocks? Stocks. Ten dollars a share for Prudentia.

Mismatched chairs and a picture of a blank-eyed Roman sculpture on the wall. A flower, though—one magnolia, browning at the fringes, pinched from a neighbor's yard and saved in a Russian Standard bottle. But wallpaper from another time, jade and chocolate in wide candy stripe. Reminded him, if the mood was just so, of a place he stayed in République as a student. Back then he was backpacking and lonely and sad. Started the holiday with a girlfriend but she decided to end it halfway so he spent the rest of Paris in physical pain at the loss. Badly in love so it was like she was dead. Genuinely had no idea what to do. Just young. Every day went down to the breakfast room and snaffled a few pastries, stood by the espresso machine drinking cup after cup before retreating back up the creaky stairs, the cold outside giving him extra reason to stay in. He made it through, though. And, anyway, a friend had drunkenly remarked that they were one of those couples that looked alike—like they had a hard-on for themselves. Kind of comment that haunts. Last thing he was was narcissistic—had other foibles, oh for sure, but never that. Anyway, made certain future lovers looked nothing like him. Bodyweight, height, hair color, skin tone, facial features—all of them had to be increasingly of the opposite end of his biological spectrum. Got weird about it. And now, alone, crippled again, by sudden, dumb loss. Things repeated, didn't they. These ups and downs were a problem that was becoming increasingly difficult to shelf. One chair from a garage sale. Another from a dead grandmother. Another, a lopsided chaise longue, left by a roommate who went to work one day and never returned. Saw him years later at the markets, weighing quinces for ripeness. The picture of the sculpture he bought in a town outside Florence. The store was unruly, smelt ancient, with objects, most of them rusting, crowding the benches. He had the sense it had been recently hauled from the ocean and left out to dry. Offended the little, bald owner somehow while becoming fixated on the print. Couldn't imagine leaving town without it. Carried it with him for the rest of his travels, manoeuvring it into overheads and luggage compartments. Now the paper was sliding out of the frame. Had resolved, after the mid-holiday break up, to adventure. Met an art collector from America on the train from Bologna to Munich. Much older than him, but she was bored or just restless and they spoke at length until she got off at Bolzano. She told him, quickly, about her brother, who she was going to see. Said he thought he was a man from a long time ago. She seemed unconcerned about it, like the news was very, very old. As the train pulled into the station, she dashed off a quick note in an unreadable scrawl. Told him she would be there for a while and to visit when he was done with Germany, which would be soon.

Forty times she's been engaged and currently she's set herself a record. Right now she's promised to eleven. It's full-time work crisscrossing the country to visit them. For weeks she'll be gone from her teeny apartment on the second floor of Knightsbridge Arms. The folks in the system must be talking, because the people at Sci Rockview and Florence State and Hiland Mountain Correctional have started razzing her: Hey, lookie here, here comes the one and only, The Great White Widow. Great White for short, apparently. If there's a lifer or some evil son-of-a-bitch on death row, she'll be sure to find him. They've got Internet sites where you can write them. Picture her typing emails through the night in that apartment of hers; things get X-rated fast, full of typos; then the visitations; then the asking for her hand in marriage. She keeps them archived and labeled in a fireproof box beneath her bed, the engagement rings. So when she does the rounds to check in with her fiancées, she'll be wearing their future on her finger. Aggravated murder, sexual battery, drug trafficking. Pokie Greene, Mateo Acosta, John Jimmy Jackson. Casting far and wide her conjugals. Lady Great White and her many sweethearts, every one of which will never make parole. "So I gotta ask, who was the first," the smart-mouthed chick checking her in at Apalachee Correctional asks.

No entry unless she answers, so she ponies up an origin story, made up on the spot since she couldn't remember, long ago as it was. "Billy," she says. "Billy Rainbow." "Billy who?" "Rainbow. All the colors and such, and at the end of it, a big fat pot of gold." "The gold's right there, girl, on your finger." So she holds it up for the guards to see through their laughter, right there, next to her middle, which she extends as well, for support. "Buuuullshit," one of the guards says. "Ok, then," she agrees: "Bullshit. Don't matter. When a man promises himself to you, it doesn't matter so much he always existed. So long as he exists for you and only you, that very moment. Now open the door."

2DIE4 on his shoulder blade. Skin salty where she kissed it, the sun drawing out his natural scent. Head rested on his forearms, turned away from her. Came out to spend a handful of moments together... Didn't know him at times. Sometimes here, sometimes not. Malik had a habit of sinking deep within himself and she still didn't know how to pull him out. Affection had worked as badly as anger. Had to find his own path through. Usually by getting in the car and driving for hours. One time didn't come home. Said he'd been at Uncle Charlie's house. They'd mixed drink with smoke and before he knew it was in no state to stay conscious let alone steer around a ton of steel, he reckoned. Waited for a couple of days before informing him she wouldn't be there when he got back if he did that again. Called Charlie *uncle* but less family and more co-conspirators—knew each other's stories. Uncle Charlie was a tough old nut but he was always kind to her. Always. Told Malik he had found someone special and to watch himself. Seemed to be Malik's voice of reason, so she left it. Bible verse on the ribs, Psalm 40:2. Ant zigzagging across his elbow, brushed it off before resettling. Walked like a criminal. Didn't know why she thought that, or what a criminal walked like. Stiff, confident, chin out. Aggressive— simple as that. But she liked it. Shouldn't have, clichéd, but did. Described him to her friend Adrienne as a spin of the wheel, where it stops, nobody knows. Adrienne eye-rolling. Hands in prayer on his bicep. Rosary beads. Dog-eared sudoku book in the grass. She opened it to where the pencil marked his page. "Hey," Malik said. "Don't finish it." Hit him with it. "Knew that would get your attention," she said. Shaded his eyes to look at her, smiled. "Nice out here," he said. "It's warm. Quiet." Turned onto his back. Still didn't know him. Didn't know his hopes and dreams. Or nightmares. Muted roaring tiger on his chest. "Tell me the last dream you had." Poked him in the ribs with the pencil. That you can remember. He thought for a moment. "This is going to sound weird. I keep having this dream, and not only when I'm sleeping. Sometimes I see it in the reflection of a window. A life, almost complete, but it isn't mine. The ups and downs. The good and the bad, almost an entire map. Like a city from above." He started to roll back over. "What do you see?" she asked. "It's me, but it's not me," he said. Left it there. The crickets and bird song and sun. Only tattoo she had was the one she got when holidaying with friends, *Good Vibes Only* ♥ in cursive on her hip.

One of the first things they'll tell her, after assigning her to One South: there's no room thirteen. If there were, it'd only make patients anxious. Had one at one time but people wigged out, begged to not be put there. So Administration nixed every room in the place that was thirteen. Room 211, 212, 214... no 13. One South was mostly addiction cases, folks one, two days off meth, heroin, spice, some combination of the three. And Xanax. Always Xanax. Her first day came to her first case to find a hulking mountain man on his hands and knees in the day room, licking the floor. Tisha, one of the techs, guessed: meth. Withdrawal from meth gets really oral. Try running Group with a bunch of folks whose nervous systems were screaming at them. Good luck! The end of her first month on One South, in came a guy who later became her favorite, legendary about the place, a homeless sweetheart who came and went on a bi-weekly basis, like most of the regulars. The psychiatrists would hold regulars as long as insurance paid for their stay; when that was no longer the case, cut them loose... in a week or two they'd be back, sure money. This guy was one of them. Mr. Thirteen they called him. Mr. Thirteen, an older case in a wheelchair, these crispy tiny ears. Said an ex of his had poured gasoline on him twenty years ago, lit him up. How else you gonna get these kinda ears? Real smiley, this guy. And each time he'd enter, he'd ask for One South; and each time during intake he'd lie, as he'd need to, claim he had a bad case of them suicidal ideations; and each time, when they agreed to take him, he'd request Room Thirteen on the unit. Miss Phillis told her: so what you'll need to do, girl, is print out a piece of paper that says in real big letters, *313*, tape it to the door of 312. Do that before techs roll him over to his room. Surely he knows it's just a piece of paper, Tanya says. Don't matter, Miss P. assures her. He appreciates the gesture, makes him happy. Why? He likes the bad luck of it. Old guy with burns on about every part of what's left of him, generous smile, more generous for the fact he's lost his teeth. Likes to know just where he's at, says Miss P. Every room here's got that number, you see. Nine, ten, twelve, don't matter. He knows as much. This whole place, just one big Thirteen. Guess you could say he's made his peace with it. And that much he'll tell you, with the smile. As if to say: here we are, in the worst. Glad I can't count and glad you're here, and can. You who keep me company.

Greyhound slim. The cheeks of a prize fighter. He loved trouble, that was obvious. This place gave him a chance and he had to tell himself daily that he needed to make the most of it. Kept his lunchtimes short and never went on smoko. Smiled in the face of the site manager when he mouthed off; the old boy had the teeth and shuffle of a drug addict, power tripping now, bossing around morons, but he was probably on chance number two here, too. Or three or four or fifteen. Anyway, kept his head down so he could crack open a beer at the end of the day and have his girl fall asleep on his chest at night. Worried in quiet moments this was all there was to life, but those thoughts led to others. Of businesses, of imports, exports. Selling things online, maybe having a space of his own. One night out with the boys, he drove home when he shouldn't have. Mentioned he was thinking about proposing so they shifted into celebration mode. Was he, though? Maybe dialing up the drinking was what he actually wanted, knew they'd oblige. The time to wake up was only a handful of hours away, he couldn't leave the truck, other excuses. Driving along and thought he was at a crossroad when he was at a T-intersection and wrapped his truck around the tree straight ahead. At speed. Catapulted. Ended up in a hedge, feeling like he'd travelled eons, confused by his sudden displacement. Like the time he woke up on the floor as a kid, having fallen off the top bunk, his brother still asleep on the bottom bed. Sat in the dark until the police came. A paramedic checked him with a flashlight and laughed when she couldn't find a scratch. "No, no," he said, there's something. Grabbed her before she could leave. "Something's happened, they did something." Stared at him blankly. "Who did?" She told him the police were taking away his licence but that was the worst of it. Home in the dawn, finally, after the final hours of the night slipped away at the police station. Took his neighbor's BMX from the garage and arrived at work dead legged and more than an hour late. Site manager called him a name he didn't recognise— displacement again. Old boy saw his confusion. "She was a skater," he said. "Other words, you're on thin ice."

Ronnie barely ate. Maybe some olives, maybe some bread or some chocolate broken into segments and forgotten, left to go chalky. Slept all morning then drank white wine late into the night. Ex-husband told her she lived like a teenager and that was her problem. Never grew up was the implication. Couldn't love by extension. Hard to convince someone it's a problem when it's not. Apartment had a water view. She watched the sky from the balcony, the lights across the river, their reflection. Thought about all the things to have come before. The times when she was the leopard-printed belle of the ball. Moments and lost loves— assuming she was capable—and things both said and not. Spent a lot of her youth clawing through brambles for happiness. Funny thing was it was there, laid out before her, but someone or thing had convinced her in whispers she needed more. Ronnie carried her sadness around like a pet, protecting and preening it, whistling to it when the days were quiet. They usually were. Yes, legs crossed, satin nightie ruffling, watched the light shimmer across the water. After the prosecco had run out and she had switched to a sappy moscato, she saw something in it. A reflection of the sky perhaps. Saw a life quivering among the lights. A figure, a man, attention's centre. The ladies drawn to him and the men trying to draw them away. A celebration or a party. A coming or a going. His friends hugging him around the neck and plying him with drink. Waiting for him to tell them what to do now. How to have fun. What to laugh at. Cheeky grin he'd had since childhood, the kid all the others wanted to be friends with, the one they'd follow into trouble. Soon, to Ronnie's delight, he was on the dancefloor, jitterbugging, lindy hopping, foxtrotting. The boy knew it all! Ronnie, glass empty, cackling, slapped her thigh in time to the beat.

The Buddhists call it *the plague of identities* but only
sometimes he's a Buddhist, more often he's a beautiful
man. Not that he'd ever need say so... his Ladies do
him the favor every Friday evening. Some carpool
together from the Home, get to Freddy Green's, club
in the basement of the Holiday Inn off Newlawn, 7:00
sharp, in their very best, their very best the very same
every Friday. Marty takes the seat before his white baby
grand, full peacock. Eighty-one-year-old darling with
ten faces (one for each lift), suited up like a Cherokee
Liberace, flowing black hair and a thin, witty little nose.
A framed photo of he and Elizabeth Taylor in the 70s,
on the grand next to flowers and flowers. The plague of
identities—who to be tonight, Peggy Lee, Rod Stewart,
Cole Porter, Journey? His Ladies sit at tables, one each,
take turns stuffing fives or tens in that empty glass at
the edge of the stage, behind him etched in the mirror,
his motto: LOVE IS FREE AND EVERTHING. Oh
babies, the plague's a pandemic now! They take turns,
stand to face the early boozers beyond the tables, gone
as old husbands at the bar. Not to sing their hearts out,
no. To sing so their hearts, years blacked out bumbling
in the wilderness, might come roaming back, prodigal
as childhood. Hardly ever answer to their own names
anymore, hearts. More often to Tin Pan Alley torch

songs reanimated by pathos-bound human breath, or, at the very least, Linda Ronstadt. Marty's fingers stumble much the way the Girls might to their rooms later, tipsy from their weekly Manhattan. The songs of their prehistory, the ballads of their youth, Marty ducking from view to suck Sativa from his vape pen; then vamping so they can call their hearts back. The songs of their future—what about those? The lyrics set in stone, the melodies: unknown. Even so, such tunes cling to memory like the classics.

Boy and mother, seated at the dinner table. Did this
thing where they invented new kingdoms. Everything
from the name and laws of the land to its culture and
currency. Mother brought out the marker pens and
paper. Boy drew an outline of the island, sometimes
the size of a fist, sometimes spanning several sheets
of paper, all with straight borders so they looked like
misshapen stars. Mother took up her coffee mug and
sat back; only now heard the rain. Dashed out the back
door, the downpour so heavy that it kicked up the dirt,
grubbying her ankles. She hurried across the yard,
tugged the sheets off the line. Already sopping. By the
time she sat back at the table, hair damp and coffee cold,
the boy had the denominations done. Circle for a five
piece, square for a ten. Triangle for a twenty, octagon
for a fifty. And the hundred was a circle with a square
hole cut where the monarch was supposed to be, like a
Chinese cash coin. "So, we know how we're paying for
bread," she said. "But what's the name of our country?"
Ignored her, tongue out, drawing the nation's flag. Boy
said he saw the world in shapes. The obvious—sun was
a circle. House a triangle on a square. Faces ovals. Most
things rectangles—some sort of quadrilateral. But then
there were other shape-things which made no sense at
all. "Alexander, what are we naming our new country?"

Learned to play violin and there were murmurs of virtuosity but he didn't want to. The dislike simple and hard, like obsidian. Mother knew, as mothers do, he could be great at a number of things, and though it was time to leave the play behind—he was outgrowing these games, becoming ungainly and awkward—she allowed it. Wanted him to remain in childhood for as long as he could, even if more and more he was looking like a big kid jammed into a small boy's world. Father texted. The boy glanced up at the bleep. Mother acknowledged with *Hurry home* and a string of black heart emojis. Put the phone down. "If you don't give it a name, Alex, I will," she said. "The king goes birdwatching," he said. "Every day, without fail." Mother raised her eyebrows. "Even on days like today?" The boy ignored her. "He takes his girlfriend out and they hunt for a purple-breasted sparrow." Mother took up some pens, a purple and a black. "The national bird?" The boy thought for a moment, finally made eye contact. "No. It's a fly-south bird. Lays its eggs along the coast, among the seals." Mother started to sketch the bird, rounder and more purple than nature would allow a migratory bird to be. "And what do the king and his girlfriend do, apart from birdwatch?" The boy averted his gaze. "Can't talk about it," he said. Mother took his hand and kissed it, then continued with her drawing of the sparrow.

Kyle Coma-Thompson is the author of the short story collections *The Lucky Body* and *Night in the Sun*. His work has been anthologized in *New American Stories* (Vintage, 2015) and *Twenty-Five Rooms* (Dostoyevsky Wannabe, 2019). He lives in Louisville, Kentucky.

Tristan Foster is a writer from Sydney, Australia. His short story collection *Letter to the Author of the Letter to the Father* was published by Transmission Press.

Sublunary Editions is a small, independent press dedicated to raising the profile of short texts from writers around the world.

For more information, please visit: sublunaryeditions.com